DISNEY
Anna & Elsa
Return to the Ice Palace

randomhousekids.com

ISBN 978-0-7364-3476-8 (hc) — ISBN 978-0-7364-8211-0 (lib. bdg.)

Printed in the United States of America

10 9 8 7 6 5 4 3 2 1

Disney
Anna & Elsa
Return to the Ice Palace

By Erica David
Illustrated by Bill Robinson,
Manuela Razzi, Francesco Legramandi,
and Gabriella Matta

Random House New York

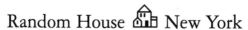

Chapter 1

Elsa peered down into the castle court-yard. From up here, at the top of the East Tower, she could see everything. She could also hear everything, from the tapping of hammers to the buzzing of saws.

Elsa stepped outside onto a narrow walkway atop the castle walls. A friendly man carrying a trowel approached her.

"The work is proceeding on schedule, Your Majesty," said the castle architect.

"Thank you, Franz," Elsa replied. It was the start of spring, and repairs were under way at Arendelle Castle. Winter had taken its toll. Stones crumbled in the castle walls, shingles dropped from rooftops, and fences lay broken in the stable yard. From where Elsa stood, she could see all the tradesmen and workers below. They swarmed back and forth across the flagstones like bees.

The door at the end of the walkway opened. Anna stepped through and hurried over to her sister.

"How's it going?" Anna asked,

pointing to the workers. "Will everything be finished before the ambassadors from Vakretta arrive?"

"It looks that way," Elsa answered.

"Remind me again why *they're* making repairs and you're not just using your frosty gifts?" said Anna, twirling her fingers in an imitation of Elsa using her powers.

"Because the castle was originally made of stone, not ice," Elsa explained.

"I kinda like your icy additions," Anna said.

"There's nothing wrong with them," Elsa agreed. "But stone is tradition. Sometimes it's nice to stick with the original."

Anna nodded. "I see what you mean," she said. "And it doesn't hurt that sticking with the original means jobs for all those workers down there."

"Exactly," Elsa replied.

Anna gave her a knowing look and said, "You are one smart queen."

"Thanks," Elsa replied. "It runs in the family."

Anna smiled. She was about to go back inside the castle, when Olaf bounded into view.

"Isn't this great?" he asked excitedly. "All these people are fixing things!"

"Olaf, is that a hammer you're carrying?" Anna inquired.

Olaf beamed with pride. He held out a small hammer.

"One of the stonemasons gave it to me," he explained. "She said I had the heart of a repairman."

"You certainly have heart," Elsa said.

"And I know just what I can fix!" Olaf cried.

Anna and Elsa exchanged a worried glance. As far as they knew, Olaf didn't know how to fix anything.

"What did you have in mind, Olaf?" Elsa asked cautiously.

"I'm glad you asked!" Olaf answered happily. "I've made a list!" The snowman held up a lengthy scroll. It was covered in drawings of broken objects throughout the castle. "Our first repair is at the grand staircase."

"*Our* first repair?" Anna asked, raising an eyebrow. "I thought *you* were the repair person."

"Well, sure," Olaf said brightly. "But we can fix things better together!"

"I have a feeling you might be right," Elsa told him, smiling. "There's just one thing."

"What's that?" the snowman asked.

"We're going to need tools, too," Elsa said with a wink.

＊

Anna, Elsa, and Olaf stood in front of the grand staircase. The wide flight of steps spiraled from the first floor to the second. The curved banister gleamed as if newly polished.

7

"The stairs look pretty good to me," Anna said. "What is it that needs to be fixed?"

"Not the stairs, the carpet," Elsa said, noticing the problem. She pointed to a rectangular rug just in front of the steps. It looked as old as the castle itself. One corner was beginning to unravel, causing the edge of the carpet to roll up. "It's a tripping hazard."

"Huh. I never noticed," Anna said.

"You wouldn't," Elsa teased playfully. "It would only trip you up on the way down. And you never go down the stairs."

Olaf looked puzzled. "Then how do you get to breakfast, Anna?" he asked. The snowman thought for a moment. "I've got it!" he said excitedly. "Magic!"

"No, Olaf. I don't have magic," Anna replied. "But I do have a little trick."

Anna climbed the staircase to the second floor. When she reached the top, she waved. "Are you ready, Olaf?" she asked.

"I'm ready!" he answered eagerly.

Anna hitched up her skirts and hopped onto the banister. On the count of three, she pushed off and slid all the way down the winding rail. When she reached the bottom of the steps, she jumped off the end just clear of the frayed carpet.

"Wow!" Olaf exclaimed. "That looks like fun. Can I try?"

"I'll go with you," Anna said.

For the next five minutes, Anna and Olaf raced up the stairs and slid down the banister. They giggled delightedly.

"You too, Elsa!" Olaf urged as he landed with a thump.

"I would, but we have a carpet to fix," Elsa reminded them.

"Oh yeah," Olaf said happily.

Anna knelt down and inspected the carpet closely.

"What should we do?" Olaf asked, propping his hands on either side of his frosty belly.

"Maybe Elsa could freeze it flat," Anna said. "It would keep the carpet from unraveling any further. It would also stop it from rolling up." She turned to her sister. "But I know you prefer not to use your magic for repairs."

"Well . . . let's try it," Elsa said. She raised her arms and swirled her fingers through the air. Tiny ice crystals formed at her fingertips. Elsa guided the icy crystals toward the carpet. Within moments, it was frozen into a flat sheet of ice.

"It's fixed!" Olaf said happily.

"Maybe we should test it out just to be sure," Anna suggested.

"Good idea," Olaf replied. He hopped up the steps, then slowly made his way back down. When he stepped off the last stair onto the frozen carpet, Olaf slipped!

"WHOOOAAAAA!" he shouted as

his feet slid out from under him. He fell down and rolled right off the rug.

Anna and Elsa rushed to help him up.

"Olaf, are you okay?" Elsa asked.

"I'm fine," he answered with a grin. "But I guess ice wasn't the best way to fix the problem."

Elsa nodded. "The thing about ice is it's slippery," she pointed out.

"You can say that again!" Olaf replied.

Anna and Elsa decided it was best to take the carpet outside to thaw. They lifted it carefully and carried it into the courtyard. Olaf helped. The three of them set the frozen rug down on the flagstones. They asked a nearby tradesman to sew up the loose threads when it thawed.

"So much for our first repair," Anna said.

"But there are still a bunch of things to fix!" Olaf declared. He looked at his list. "Aha! Next stop, the library!"

Elsa looked at Anna. Anna shrugged. *What could possibly need Olaf's attention in the library?* they wondered. Nonetheless, they followed in the snowman's footsteps as he bounded happily back indoors.

Chapter 2

Anna, Elsa, and Olaf stared up at the two large oak doors that opened into the castle library. They were firmly closed. Their shiny brass handles winked in the light of the corridor. Nothing but silence came from the other side.

"What's the trouble here, Olaf?" Anna asked.

Instead of answering, Olaf provided a demonstration. He turned a handle and pulled open one of the doors. A long squeak sang out from the metal hinges.

"That's pretty loud," Elsa said. "It would definitely distract anyone trying to read, especially our guests from Vakretta."

"And this is a library!" Olaf pointed out. "Its middle name is *shhhh*!"

Anna opened the second door. *SQUEEEEAK!* The sound was almost musical. Olaf noticed it, too. He moved his door just a hair. A shorter squeak followed Anna's drawn-out sound. They moved their doors at the same time. Two squeaks rang out in unison. Soon they were playing a squeaky symphony.

Squee squee squee squee squeeeak!

Squeak SQUEAK!

Squeak SQUEAK!

Squee squee squee squee squeeeak!

Squeak SQUEAK!

Squeak SQUEAK!

"Ahem!" Elsa said, interrupting the squeaky-door orchestra and trying not to laugh. "I thought we were going to *stop* the squeaks, not make more."

"Sorry," Anna replied. She and Olaf let go of the doors.

"What do you think, Mr. Fix-It?" Anna said to Olaf.

The snowman shrugged.

"We could oil the hinges," Elsa said. "That would probably stop the noise."

Olaf liked that idea. "I know where we can get oil," he said, and scampered off down the hall. A few minutes later, he returned holding an oil can. It looked just like a teakettle but with a long, skinny spout. "I borrowed it," he explained.

Anna, Elsa, and Olaf stepped into the library and closed the doors behind them. Olaf oiled the door hinges—at least, the ones he could reach.

"Boost me up!" he said to Anna and Elsa. They lifted him so he could oil the hinges near the top of each door.

Once all the hinges were oiled, Olaf turned the door handles. He was eagerly anticipating the wonderful sound of silence. But there was one small problem.

19

"The doors are stuck!" Olaf exclaimed.

"What do you mean, they're stuck?" Anna asked incredulously. She tried both of the doors herself. They didn't budge.

"What happened?" Elsa asked. "Oiling the hinges should have made them open more easily."

Anna picked up Olaf's oil can. The metal was old and slightly rusty. She could barely make out the letters on the side.

"'G' . . . 'L' . . . 'U' . . . 'E' . . . Olaf! This isn't oil, it's glue!" she cried.

"Oops," Olaf mumbled. "Wrong can."

Elsa tried the doors, too, and got the same result. They were well and truly stuck in the library—just Anna, Elsa, Olaf, and hundreds of books.

Elsa and Anna thumped their hands against the doors. They called out in the hope that someone walking by might hear them. Olaf shouted, too.

"Helloooo?" he said. "Is anyone out there? We're trapped!"

Five minutes went by and no one heard them.

"It looks like we're going to be here for a while," Elsa pointed out.

"At least there's plenty to read!" Olaf said optimistically. He looked up at the tall shelves full of books. "If only I knew how."

Anna didn't feel much like reading, however. She had a better idea. "Elsa, maybe your magic can get us out of here," she said.

"How?" Elsa asked. "It didn't work so well on the carpet."

"I know!" Olaf chimed in excitedly. "Make a blizzard in the library. Everyone will come running!"

"Hmm," Elsa said, considering. "I'm not sure that's the best idea. For starters, it will be very cold, and the snow might damage the books."

"I was thinking you could just freeze the hinges," Anna said. "Once the metal is cold enough, it'll be brittle. Then we can smash the doors open."

"That just might work," Elsa said. She summoned her frosty magic and aimed a chilly blast at the door hinges. The metal groaned as it froze. When she was finished, each hinge was covered in a small, icy mound.

Anna walked over to the bookshelves. She found the biggest book she could carry. It was a heavy encyclopedia. "This oughta do it," she said, lugging the book over to the doors.

"Is it story time already?" Olaf asked.

"Not quite," Anna replied. "I'm going

to use this book to break the hinges!"

Anna lifted the big book and swung. *SMASH!* The first hinge cracked and fell to the floor in pieces.

Elsa couldn't help smiling. "Is that as fun as it looks?" she asked.

"More," Anna answered. "Wanna try?"

Elsa pushed up the sleeves of her gown. She took the heavy book from Anna and let the second hinge have it. *WHAM!*

"Wow!" said Olaf. "You smashed it to smithereens! My turn!"

Olaf could barely lift the enormous book in his tiny twig arms. Anna and Elsa helped him. Together, they smashed the remaining hinges. *WHAM! BAM!*

With the hinges gone, there was

nothing to hold the doors in place. Anna reached out and tapped the door on the left. It tipped over and hit the floor with a resounding *CRASH!*

Giggling, Elsa pushed the second door. It crashed to the floor with a *THUD!*

"We're free!" Olaf said in delight, but his celebration was interrupted by the sound of footsteps.

Kai, Anna and Elsa's loyal servant, came racing down the hall. "What's all that noise?" he asked worriedly. "Is everyone okay?"

"Better than okay!" Olaf answered.

"Now that we're out of the library," Anna chimed in.

Elsa apologized for all the noise. "We

were just trying to help with the repairs," she explained.

Kai looked at the empty space where the library doors used to be. "With all due respect, Your Majesty, I think you just created another repair," he said.

Elsa sighed. "Yes. Please extend my apologies to the builders," she said. "And let them know we'll need a new set of hinges."

Kai bowed politely and left to find the castle architect.

Chapter 3

"Maybe we should leave the repairs to the professionals," Anna said as she, Elsa, and Olaf stepped over the fallen doors.

"But the royal chef needs our help!" Olaf told her. "It's the next thing on my list."

"The royal chef?" Elsa asked. "Is something wrong in the kitchen?"

Olaf nodded. "And if we don't help, she won't be ready for the visitors from Vakretta."

Elsa and Anna followed Olaf into the kitchen. The royal chef and her assistants were preparing for the ambassadors from Vakretta. That meant two extra mouths to feed at breakfast, lunch, and dinner. And they were very important mouths. Elsa hoped to impress her guests during their stay at the castle. It was a chance to improve the trade relationship between the two kingdoms.

The chef knew that everything had to be perfect. That was why the leaky water pump in the kitchen had her so worried.

"It's really slowing us down," said the

chef, pointing to the pump. A steady stream of water leaked from a small crack at the base. "We're spending too much time mopping up puddles!"

Olaf hopped to attention. He bounded over to the water pump to inspect the leak. "The crack isn't that big." He reached out with his branchlike hand and covered the crack with one finger. "There!" he exclaimed.

Anna and Elsa looked at each other, concerned. Olaf had definitely plugged the leak, but it didn't seem like a permanent solution.

"That's great, Olaf," Elsa said gently. "But you can't just stand there forever with your finger on the pump."

"I don't mind," Olaf replied cheerfully. "I love the kitchen."

"Right, but who will help greet our visitors when they arrive?" Anna asked.

Olaf considered the question. Greeting castle guests was one of his favorite things, but the kitchen really needed him. It was a tough choice. He frowned. "You and Elsa can handle that," he said reluctantly.

"Are you sure? I mean, who will give our guests warm hugs?" Anna said slyly. She knew she could tempt the snowman with the mention of warm hugs.

Olaf couldn't contain his excitement. He was absolutely born to hug people! "*I WILL!*" he blurted out. In his enthusiasm, he let go of the pump. Water rushed out, creating a new puddle on the floor. "Whoops!"

"That's okay," Elsa replied. "I think I have a way to fix the pump."

"Does it involve frosty goodness?" Anna teased her lightheartedly.

"Of course!" Elsa channeled her magic toward the pump. In seconds, she'd frozen the crack at the base. The leak was fixed. "It's just a temporary solution," she explained. "We'll need the plumbers to come see it before it melts."

"Thank you, Your Majesty!" the royal chef said with a sigh of relief. "Now we can get back to more important things."

"Like gooey chocolate nougat with fresh lingonberries?" asked Anna.

"Like gooey chocolate nougat with fresh lingonberries," agreed the chef.

Anna, Elsa, and Olaf left the kitchen.

"We did it!" Olaf said as they walked down the corridor. "We fixed something!"

"I'm proud of us," said Anna.

"Me too," Elsa told them.

They were surprised, then, when two hours later, a cry went up from the kitchen. Kai was once again on the run. This time, he knocked urgently at the door to Elsa's study. Elsa and Anna were chatting quietly about the upcoming visit from the ambassadors, while Olaf listened eagerly.

"Come in," Elsa said.

Kai hurried into the room. "Your Majesty," he said breathlessly, "there's plumbing trouble in the kitchen!"

Anna, Elsa, and Olaf rushed back to the kitchen with Kai. When they got there, they saw water everywhere! It gushed rapidly from the base of the water pump.

"What happened?" Anna asked.

"I don't know!" said the chef, frustrated.

She was at her wits' end. "But how am I supposed to cook like this?"

"Uh-oh," Elsa said. "Maybe I caused it."

"But you stopped the leak," Olaf pointed out.

"I'll bet one of the pipes burst when I froze the pump," Elsa said. With the winter they'd just had, it was entirely possible.

"Now what?" Olaf asked.

Elsa focused on the water flooding the floor. She wound her fingers through the air and created a flurry of frost. The frost swirled over the surface of the water, causing it to harden into ice.

"Oooooh, pretty!" Olaf whispered in awe.

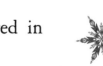

Elsa molded the ice into a beautiful sculpture. As the ice took shape, the sculpture became easier to recognize.

"It's Chef!" said Anna, pointing to the statue's familiar features.

The royal chef was so flattered she forgot all about being frustrated. She stared at the ice sculpture and smiled in delight.

Gently, Kai cleared his throat. "Shall I call the repair people, Your Majesty?" he asked.

"Please," Elsa said humbly. "And tell them I'm giving them a raise."

Chapter 4

The next morning, Olaf got up early. He couldn't wait to start another day of fixing things. The fact that he, Anna, and Elsa had frozen a carpet, knocked down the library doors, and caused a flood in the kitchen didn't slow him down one bit.

"Anna, Elsa, I'm ready!" he called from the bottom of the grand staircase.

Anna and Elsa went down to meet him.

"You won't be needing your hammer today," Anna told Olaf.

"Why not?" Olaf asked.

"Today we'll be making a different kind of fix," Anna replied. She led Olaf from the stairs to a small alcove in the main hallway. There, Anna opened a door. A mountain of broken furniture, old toys, and other odd items tumbled out.

"Some parts of the castle are far too cluttered," Elsa explained, joining them.

"What is this?" Olaf asked curiously.

"Some are gifts," Anna said. Every week the villagers met with Elsa in the audience chamber to ask her advice. As Queen of Arendelle, it was Elsa's duty to help solve their problems. Elsa loved helping them—and she was good at it, too. The townspeople were so pleased that they brought her gifts. The only trouble was that there were a lot of gifts.

"Others are old toys," Elsa said. She picked up a dusty teddy bear from the pile.

"And the rest of these things belong to you," Anna said to Olaf. She knelt down and pulled a wooden chest from the jumble of objects. The lid was stamped PROPERTY OF OLAF.

"Hey! It's my special collection!" Olaf said happily. "I've been looking for that!"

"It probably got lost in this giant pile of stuff," Anna remarked.

Olaf took the chest from Anna and set it down on the floor. He lifted the lid and peeked inside. "It's all still here!" he said excitedly.

"What's in your collection, Olaf?" Elsa asked.

"Oh, you know, the usual," the snowman replied. He began to pull his special treasures out of the box. There were pinecones, fish bones, and buttons of all shapes and sizes. There was a collection of string and a set of decorative pie plates. There were pebbles and oddly shaped stones. It looked like Olaf collected anything and everything.

"It's time for some of these old things to find new homes," Elsa said.

Olaf's eyes brightened at the thought. "I love giving things new homes!"

*

Later that afternoon, Anna, Elsa, and Olaf stood in front of an enormous mound of stuff. They'd sorted the doohickeys from the doodads and the odds from the ends. The result was one huge pile of donations.

"How did we get so much stuff?" Anna asked, astonished. She knew that most of the items had built up over the years, but to see everything at once was shocking.

Elsa shook her head, exhausted. She, Anna, and Olaf had emptied every chest,

wardrobe, and closet they could find. They would keep some things, donate others, and reluctantly let go of the rest.

Olaf was particularly proud of himself. He was giving away almost his entire collection, except for one decorative pie plate. There was a jolly little snowman on the front. The resemblance to Olaf was astounding.

Elsa brushed a lock of hair from her face. "I think I learned a lesson," she said. "If we do this more often, we won't have to sort through so much."

"Does that mean we get to do this all the time?" asked Olaf. His eyes sparkled with excitement. He took his job very seriously.

"Not all the time," Elsa answered. "But maybe once a month."

"There's another option, you know," Anna said.

"What's that?" Elsa asked.

"We could just get a bigger place. Then we would have room for more treasures," Anna replied, winking at Olaf.

Elsa smiled and folded her arms across

her chest. "We have enough on our hands trying to repair *this* place," she said. "A bigger castle is out of the question."

Elsa called for Kai to help pack up the donations. The servant arrived with an unexpected guest. Kristoff stood beside him, breathing heavily. The mountain man wiped a line of sweat from his brow. It was clear that he'd just raced to the castle.

"You'll never guess what I saw!" Kristoff said quickly.

"Well, hello to you, too," Anna teased him.

Kristoff smiled sheepishly. He waved hello to everyone before launching into his story. "I was riding in my sleigh, which I had *just* polished, by the way. I was making an ice delivery, but Sven was dragging his hooves, and I had just turned onto Ragnor's Pass because I know a great shortcut—"

Kristoff stopped and looked at Anna, Elsa, and Olaf. They were staring at their rambling friend, wondering where he was going with his story.

"The point is, I saw this big . . . ice thing, and it was floating along in a stream of melting snow from the North Mountain!"

"A big ice thing? I love big ice things!" Olaf blurted out.

"Just what *is* this big ice thing?" Elsa asked.

"That's just it," Kristoff said. "I don't know, but it looked like part of an ice sculpture or something."

"Do you think it's something Elsa made?" Anna asked.

"I was hoping you'd tell me," Kristoff replied with a shrug. He invited Anna, Elsa, and Olaf to go with him into the mountains. There, they could see the mysterious "big ice thing" for themselves.

Chapter 5

Kristoff led Elsa, Anna, and Olaf up a winding mountain path. As they walked along the trail, it grew steeper and steeper. Olaf huffed and puffed as he climbed. With his little legs, he had to work extra hard to keep up with the others.

The four friends followed a running stream of clear, cold water. It trickled down from the mountaintop. The stream was made from melting snow. It burbled along, carrying bits and pieces of ice from high up in the mountains.

Anna drew her cloak tight against the chill. Though it was springtime in Arendelle, the tops of the tallest mountains were still snowy. The higher she climbed with Kristoff, Elsa, and Olaf, the colder it got.

"Not much farther now," Kristoff said. He hiked the last few feet over a gentle rise and pointed. "There it is!" he exclaimed.

A large piece of ice bobbed slowly on the surface of the stream. It glittered like crystal in the midday sun. As the current pushed it closer, Anna recognized it.

49

"Elsa, does that look familiar to you?" she asked.

"It sure does," Elsa answered. It was a fragment of the beautiful ice chandelier from her palace on the North Mountain.

Elsa hadn't been to the North Mountain in quite some time. Being queen kept her very busy in Arendelle. She counted on Marshmallow, the friendly snow monster, to watch over the ice palace. Marshmallow's job had become a lot more exciting once the mischievous little snowmen known as snowgies had moved in.

"Is it from your ice palace?" Kristoff asked, pointing to the bobbing ice.

Elsa nodded and told them about the chandelier.

Kristoff frowned. "Correct me if I'm wrong, but the last time I saw the chandelier, it was in one piece," he said.

"Hmmm," Elsa replied, suddenly worried about Marshmallow and the snowgies. "Maybe it's time to pay the ice palace a visit."

*

A short while later, Elsa, Anna, Kristoff, and Olaf arrived at the ice palace. The enormous structure stood at the very top of the North Mountain. It was just as impressive as Anna remembered, with its frozen towers and tall, pointed spires made of ice. To reach the entrance, the four friends climbed a steep bridge of frosty stairs. When they stood before the grand entrance, Elsa opened the front doors to a gust of chilly air.

Marshmallow was the first to meet them. The giant snow monster lumbered into the Great Hall. He smiled wide in greeting.

"Hi, Marshmallow!" Olaf said brightly.

Marshmallow rumbled in response. He leaned down to pat Olaf gently on the head.

"Is everything okay here, Marshmallow?" Elsa asked. "We saw part of the chandelier floating downstream."

Marshmallow pointed to the other half

of the chandelier. It dangled dangerously
from the ceiling. The snow monster
launched into a slow pantomime. Everyone watched him closely.

"I think he tripped over something and
accidentally knocked into the chandelier,"
Elsa said, interpreting Marshmallow's

gestures. The snow monster leaped from foot to foot as if he were walking over hot coals.

"Not just something, but lots of little *somethings,* from the looks of it," Anna said, watching Marshmallow hop up and down.

Suddenly, Anna, Elsa, Kristoff, and Olaf heard the pitter-patter of teeny-tiny snowy feet. A tide of snowgies poured into the Great Hall. They spilled into the room, one after another and another and another and another . . .

"Hi, Flake, and Fridge, and Flurry, and Powder, and Crystal, and Slush, and Sludge . . . ," Olaf greeted them cheerfully.

"Olaf, do you have names for every

single one of them?" Anna asked.

"Of course! And Blizzard, and Blitz, and Glacier, and Freeze, and Frost . . . ," Olaf continued, without missing a beat.

The snowgies filled the room with the sound of their tapping feet. There were so many of them that they practically carpeted the floor! It was no wonder Marshmallow had tripped over them and accidentally broken the chandelier.

Anna was delighted to see the snowgies again. She hadn't seen them since her last birthday, when Elsa had unintentionally sneezed them to life. Anna scooped up an armful of the tiny snowmen and hugged them to her chest.

"Hi, guys," she said.

Elsa laughed happily as a flock of snowgies gathered around her. They smiled up at her and hopped onto her dress, hoping to catch a ride on the hem of her gown. Elsa twirled and the snowgies squealed gleefully as they clung to her dress.

Kristoff did his best to ignore the mischievous little snowmen. He'd spent more than his fair share of time chasing after them on Anna's birthday. But even he couldn't resist their charms. One look into their impish coal-black eyes and he had to crack a smile.

When Olaf was finally done greeting the snowgies, he looked up at the chandelier. It was clearly in need of repair.

"I found something that needs fixing," he announced cheerfully. "Where did I put my tool belt?"

"Let me handle this one, Olaf," Elsa said gently. "This time, I'm confident that using ice will work." With a whirl of her fingers, she directed a delicate stream of ice at the chandelier. Tiny crystals of frost swirled around the jagged, broken edges. Slowly, Elsa rebuilt the chandelier. When she was done, it looked like a cross between a shimmering snowflake and a shooting star. Thin branches of ice radiated from the center. They were engraved with a delicate curlicue design.

"Wow!" Anna gasped. "Elsa, it's beautiful."

The new chandelier seemed to shine with a light all its own. Even the snowgies stood still, mesmerized by the glow. The entire room looked different.

"It's like a whole new palace!" Olaf exclaimed, basking in the light.

"Hey, that's it!" Anna said. Her eyes lit up with the spark of a brand-new idea. "I was just saying we should get a bigger place. Now we have one!"

Elsa raised an eyebrow. "Just what are you up to, Anna?" she asked. "We're donating your treasures, not keeping them here."

"Not the treasures, the ambassadors!" Anna said. "We can host them here!"

With all the excitement, Elsa had

almost forgotten about the visitors from Vakretta. "I don't know, Anna," she said uncertainly. "This place was never meant to host important guests. It was just for . . . me."

"But it's fantastic! There's nothing like it anywhere in the world! I'm sure our guests would be honored to see it," Anna told her.

"You think so?" asked Elsa.

"I know so," Anna replied.

"Well, I guess I could make it a little more comfortable," Elsa said, warming up to the idea.

Olaf celebrated with a delighted whoop. The snowgies circled him and began jumping up and down with excitement.

"Ahem," Kristoff spoke up, clearing his throat. "Aren't you two forgetting something?"

Anna gave him a questioning look.

"Who's going to keep an eye on these guys?" he asked, pointing to the tiny snowmen.

Before Elsa or Anna could answer, Olaf volunteered.

"I will!" he shouted happily.

"Problem solved," Anna responded. She waded through the sea of snowgies and took her sister's arm.

"This is going to be one state visit the ambassadors from Vakretta will never forget!" she said.

Chapter 6

The next morning, Elsa, Anna, Kristoff, and Olaf set to work on the ice palace. They had just two days until the Vakrettans arrived. Elsa had come up with a number of ways to prepare the icy castle for their guests. First, they would need furniture. Most of the rooms were empty.

"I can use my powers to make furniture

out of ice," Elsa explained to everyone.

"That will go nicely with the rest of the frosty decor," Anna said. "But do you have time to do that with everything else you have planned?"

"I think I can be of assistance," Kristoff told them. "After all, I am a professional ice harvester. I can carve anything out of ice."

"Really? Because I've only seen you carve blocks out of ice," Anna teased him.

"Yes, and those blocks are perfectly . . . blocky," Kristoff proudly replied.

Elsa decided to take Kristoff up on his offer. Together, they drew up a plan for a beautiful dining table and a set of chairs carved out of ice. Kristoff gathered his ice-carving tools and set to work. With his help, Elsa was free to make other improvements.

Next, Elsa and Anna took a walk outside. They looked over the palace, inspecting it for cracks. Some of the spires and towers had been damaged by the strong mountain winds and weather. Elsa used her powers to repair any dents and scratches. When she was finished, the outside of the palace looked like new. The icy turrets glittered against the bright blue sky.

Inside the palace, Olaf made good on his promise to keep an eye on the snowgies. In fact, he did more than keep an eye on

them. "Gather round, little brothers. You too, Marshmallow!" he said, calling everyone to attention. "The ambassadors are very important guests, and we need to make them feel welcome."

Olaf figured he knew all about what to do—or rather, what *not* to do—when important guests came to visit. Each time Anna and Elsa hosted dignitaries at Arendelle Castle, he'd learned a new rule of etiquette. Etiquette meant polite behavior. For example, it was polite to greet people first, before leaping into their arms for warm hugs.

"The best way to make people feel welcome is to greet them with a bow," Olaf said. He leaned forward from the middle of his frosty belly until the tip of his carrot nose touched the ground. Then he snapped upright again. "You try it," he said, pointing to Marshmallow.

The giant snow monster looked uncertain. He placed his icy hands on his

hips and tilted forward. His enormous body wobbled as he bent toward the floor. It was an awkward position for such a large creature. To the tiny snowgies, it looked like a mountain was about to fall on them! They scattered in all directions across the Great Hall.

"Come back!" Olaf cried after them.

Marshmallow finished bowing. He stood and smiled apologetically at the little snowmen. They peeped out at him from the corners of the room. When they were sure the snow monster was steady on his feet, they crept forward again.

"That was great, Marshmallow!" Olaf said encouragingly. "Keep practicing."

Marshmallow smiled. He clomped out of the room, bowing clumsily as he went.

"I've got something special planned for you guys," Olaf told the snowgies. "It's kind of fancy, but you can handle it."

Olaf organized the little snowmen into a straight line. It wasn't as easy as it sounded. The snowgies were full of energy. They liked to wriggle and fidget, but finally Olaf got them lined up. There were so many of them that the line stretched from one end of the Great Hall to the other.

Carefully, Olaf explained his plan. When he gave the signal, the snowgies would jump, one after the other, starting with the first snowman in line. From

a distance, it would look like one big welcome wave.

"Everybody ready?" Olaf called.

The snowgies blinked up at him expectantly.

Olaf waved his arms and gave the signal. But instead of an orderly wave, there was complete chaos! The tiny snowmen hopped up and down and up and down and up and down! They bounced all over the place, scrambling across the Great Hall.

"Little brothers!" Olaf shouted, but the snowgies didn't listen.

After a couple of minutes, the little snowmen began to flock together. Before

Olaf knew it, the snowgies swarmed toward him!

"Uh-oh," he said.

The snowgies charged Olaf and swept him off his feet!

Outside the ice palace, Anna and Elsa had just finished another repair when the front doors flew open. A wave of snowgies poured out, carrying Olaf on their heads. "Put me down!" Olaf giggled. "We've got work to do!"

But the snowgies had a different idea. They carried Olaf off to play in the snow.

"What on earth?" Elsa asked as a huge gaggle of snowgies passed by carrying the snowman.

"I have no idea," Anna replied, shaking her head and smiling.

"Should we be worried?" said Elsa.

"No," Anna answered lightly. "If I know Olaf, they'll be back in plenty of time for bed."

Chapter 7

Two days later, the ice palace was ready to receive its first official visitors. Anna and Elsa dressed in their finest gowns and walked through the frozen corridors. Each room they passed had been decorated with beautiful furniture made of ice. In the Great Hall stood Kristoff's impressive hand-carved dining table and chairs. The icy tabletop shone like glass, reflecting the restored chandelier that hung from the ceiling.

"It's breathtaking," Anna said, glancing around the room.

Elsa had also had carpets, pillows, and tapestries brought from Arendelle Castle. She thought it would help to make the ice palace more comfortable.

"I hope the ambassadors like it," Elsa said.

"Of course they will," Anna reassured her.

Elsa wrung her hands, eager to make sure everything was going as planned. She crossed the room and poked her head into

a small chamber next to the Great Hall. The royal chef and her assistants were hard at work, making dinner for the Vakrettan guests. Since there were no ovens in the ice palace, the chef was preparing a delicious menu of chilled foods. She was excited to present them to the ambassadors.

Elsa turned back to Anna and smoothed her dress nervously.

"It'll be fine," Anna told her.

Suddenly, Olaf burst into the Great Hall. "They're here!" he shouted exuberantly.

Anna and Elsa followed Olaf outside. They took their places next to Kristoff and Marshmallow, who were already

awaiting the ambassadors. The Vakrettans arrived in an elegant horse-drawn sleigh. Ambassador Mitya and Ambassador Galina had taken a long journey to reach Arendelle. They'd traveled across the sea by boat, over land on reindeer back, and finally into the mountains by sleigh.

Mitya and Galina climbed down from their sleigh and walked across the snow to greet Elsa and Anna.

"Pleased to meet you, Your Majesty," Mitya said, bowing. He wore a thick coat to protect him from the mountain cold.

"Welcome to Arendelle," Elsa said, smiling brightly.

Ambassador Galina curtseyed in her

77

heavy fur cloak. "It's a pleasure to be here," she said. "We've heard of Arendelle Castle, but this place is incredible. Is it made entirely of ice?"

"Yes," Elsa replied.

"Elsa made it herself," Anna said, with a nod toward her sister.

Elsa introduced Anna, Kristoff, and Olaf to the ambassadors. Olaf was careful to follow the rules of etiquette. He waited until after he was introduced to ask for warm hugs.

Warm hugs from a snowman were a new experience for Galina and Mitya. Though Vakretta had similar weather to Arendelle, it had totally different snowmen. None of

the snowmen in Vakretta walked, talked, or hugged. In fact, there was no other snowman quite like Olaf anywhere.

Mitya and Galina were in for a number of new experiences in Arendelle. Their second new experience took one lumbering step toward them. Marshmallow was the last to be introduced.

"May I present Marshmallow," Elsa said. "He watches over the ice palace."

The ambassadors reeled back in surprise. The giant snow monster had been standing so still, they thought he was a statue. They were even more shocked when the creature placed his hands on his hips and leaned forward unsteadily.

"What's he doing?" Mitya whispered
to Galina.

"I think he's greeting us," Galina
replied quietly. "Maybe it's a special snow
creature custom." Ambassadors Mitya and
Galina decided to return the greeting.

They bent forward with their hands on their hips and wobbled clumsily.

Marshmallow seemed pleased. He had practiced his bow for two whole days. He took the ambassadors' greeting as a sign of encouragement and bowed even deeper. The trouble was, the deeper he bowed, the clumsier he became. The huge snow monster lost his balance!

Marshmallow stumbled toward the ambassadors. Momentum carried him forward at a rapid pace.

"Look out!" Mitya shouted. He was afraid that he and Galina were about to be accidentally crushed by a snow giant!

Galina's eyes widened in alarm. She

grabbed Mitya by the collar of his coat and got ready to jump out of the way. But before she could make a move, Elsa leaped into action.

The queen focused her magic on Marshmallow. Frost swirled around her. With a flick of her wrist, Elsa surrounded Marshmallow with a wall of ice. He was held in place by the sturdy walls.

The ambassadors breathed a sigh of relief.

"Phew! That was close," Anna said.

"Are you all right?" Elsa asked her guests, concerned.

"We're fine," Mitya replied quickly.

Marshmallow rumbled an apology and the ambassadors nodded.

"Well, now that everyone's been introduced, why don't we head inside?" Anna said. Olaf leaped to attention and led the ambassadors toward the bridge of frosty stairs. Kristoff followed, and Anna and Elsa brought up the rear.

As they climbed the stairs, Elsa gave Anna an apprehensive look.

"What's wrong?" Anna whispered.

"Let's just say that wasn't the perfect welcome I'd pictured," Elsa answered. In spite of her best efforts, things had gotten off to a slightly shaky start.

Chapter 8

Olaf pushed open the doors to the Great Hall. He enthusiastically ushered the ambassadors inside. Everything was set for his welcome wave with the snowgies. A wide curtain had been hung across the middle of the hall. Behind it, the snowgies were all lined up and ready to salute the guests.

"Have a seat, everyone!" Olaf said eagerly.

Anna, Elsa, Mitya, and Galina sat in front of the curtain. Then Olaf took up his position to the side. He raised his hands in the air like an orchestra conductor. The snowman nodded to Kristoff, who pulled on a rope to drop the curtain. The curtain fell to the floor. For Olaf, it was the moment he'd been waiting for. That was why he was so surprised to see that the snowgies weren't there! The space behind the curtain was empty!

"Uh-oh," Anna said to Elsa. "Why do I get the feeling this wasn't supposed to happen?"

Elsa gave an embarrassed smile. To

her, it seemed like nothing was going as planned.

The ambassadors stared curiously. "Could it be another Arendelle custom?" Mitya whispered to Galina. Galina shrugged uncertainly. She had no idea what to make of the emptiness behind the curtain.

Anna wasn't sure where the snowgies had gone, but she wanted to keep Olaf's promise of a welcome surprise. Quickly, she came up with a new idea.

"Ladies and gentlemen, may I present to you Kristoff the Magnificent!" Anna announced.

Kristoff was still holding the curtain rope. He looked up at Anna, utterly

confused. Anna ran over to Kristoff and drew him into the middle of the floor. All eyes were on the ice harvester. He waved nervously to the ambassadors. Though he'd been introduced to them earlier, he was suddenly shy.

"That's right, ladies and gentlemen, Kristoff here is the strongest man in Arendelle," Anna said sunnily.

"I am?" Kristoff asked.

"He is?" Elsa and Olaf said at the same time.

Anna nodded.

"I mean, of course I am," Kristoff said confidently. He didn't know exactly what Anna had in mind, but he liked the sound of Kristoff the Magnificent.

"For his first display of strength, watch as Kristoff lifts . . . Olaf!" Anna cried. Delighted, Olaf took a running leap and landed in the ice harvester's arms. Playing along, Kristoff lifted Olaf above his head. "Don't let Olaf's appearance fool you," Anna said. "He may look as light as a snowflake, but he's heavier than an avalanche!"

The ambassadors applauded politely. Kristoff set Olaf down and bowed to the audience. He was beginning to like his role as the strongest man in Arendelle.

"Now Princess Anna!" Olaf said eagerly.

Neither Anna nor Elsa thought that was a good idea. Elsa rose to her feet. Before Kristoff reached Anna, she cleared her throat. "Actually, that's all the time we have for Kristoff the Magnificent," Elsa said. "Dinner is served."

Anna was relieved. She winked secretly at Elsa, congratulating her on her quick thinking. Kristoff and Olaf didn't seem to mind the interruption. They volunteered to escort Mitya and Galina to the dining area.

Once the ambassadors were seated in their beautifully carved ice chairs, Elsa signaled to the chef to serve the meal. Footmen emerged from the small chamber next to the Great Hall, carrying delicious cold dishes.

"We're delighted to have you here," Elsa told the ambassadors.

"Thank you, Your Majesty. The people of Vakretta send you their best regards," Galina replied formally.

"We still remember the time you helped us during our unbearably warm summer," Mitya said.

"I love summer!" Olaf said cheerfully.

"You may not have loved this one," Mitya explained. "It was far too hot."

Elsa smiled at the memory. She and Anna had visited Vakretta last year. At the time, the village was in the middle of a heat wave. Elsa had conjured a refreshing flurry to keep everyone cool.

"I was happy to help," Elsa said. "And we can supply you with ice anytime."

"I can see that," Mitya replied, staring in wonder at the icy corridors around him.

Elsa spoke to the ambassadors about importing ice from Arendelle. In exchange, Vakretta would send some of its finest hand-woven lace. As they discussed the trade, Elsa didn't notice the three snowgies creeping into the Great Hall.

The tiny snowmen scampered over to the dining table. Gleefully, they shimmied up one of the table legs and climbed onto the top. The table was set with fancy plates, glasses, and serving dishes. The snowgies scrambled in and out of the elegant tableware, playing a game of hide-and-seek. They were so quiet that no one spotted them.

One little snowman hopped into a large tureen of chilled fish soup. It was the perfect hiding spot until Anna reached for the ladle. She didn't see the snowgie swimming in the large serving dish. As a result, she almost scooped him into her bowl!

The tiny snowman narrowly escaped.

He climbed out of the tureen, hopped down onto the table, and hurried to find another hiding place. Unfortunately, he ran straight into a glass of water. It tipped over with a splash!

Anna was surprised to see the overturned water glass next to her plate. She didn't remember knocking it over. Even stranger, no one saw her go anywhere near the glass. But she must have touched it somehow.

"I'm sorry," she apologized courteously to the dinner guests. Anna picked up a napkin to mop up the spill. Before she could wipe up the water, however, it froze to the tabletop—one of the benefits of dining on a table made out of ice.

93

Meanwhile, the three snowgies climbed down to the floor and darted beneath the table. They zigzagged between the dinner guests' feet, past Elsa's sparkly heels, Anna's sturdy slippers, Kristoff's lug-soled boots, and the ambassadors' travel shoes. The snowgies saw the shoes as an obstacle course. They leaped over lug soles, slid under slippers, and hopped over high heels in sheer delight.

Elsa continued her conversation with Galina and Mitya. "Is there anything special you'd like to see during your stay in Arendelle?" she asked.

"Yes. I heard you have a famous trading post," Galina answered.

"Wandering Oaken's Trading Post and Sauna. I'm sure Oaken would love to meet you," Anna chimed in. "What about you, Ambassador Mitya?"

"I would like to visit your frozen lake and see the ice harvest," he told her. Suddenly, Mitya sat straight up in his chair, startled.

"Is everything all right?" Elsa asked.

"Something just brushed my foot," Mitya explained. "You don't by any chance have pets?"

Anna peeked under the table to investigate. She was greeted by the sight of three snowgies bouncing playfully on the toe of Mitya's shoe.

"Shoo!" Anna whispered fiercely. The snowgies scattered at the sound of her voice.

Anna looked up to meet Elsa's questioning gaze.

"Um, we don't have pets," Anna told Mitya. "But we do have a snowgie problem," she said, lowering her voice so that only Elsa could hear. Elsa's eyes widened.

Elsa knew they had to do something about the snowgies. Left to their own devices, they always ended up making mischief. She put down her fork and knife and stood. "I'm going to check with the chef about dessert," she said, inventing an

excuse. "Kristoff, Anna, would you mind helping me?"

Anna stood to follow her, but Kristoff remained in his chair. "Do I have to?" he asked through a mouthful of food. "I'm still eating."

"Yes, you have to," Anna said firmly, nudging him with her elbow. She turned to the ambassadors. "Please excuse us. We won't be a moment."

Reluctantly, Kristoff rose from his seat. He followed Elsa and Anna into the chef's chamber, where Elsa came up with a plan.

Chapter 9

Elsa's plan was this: She and Olaf would continue to entertain the ambassadors. Meanwhile, Kristoff and Anna would go on a secret hunt to round up the snowgies and keep them out of the Great Hall. That was easier said than done, however. There were so many of them, and they were everywhere! The tiny snowmen scampered in and out of the palace's frosty rooms. They hid behind tapestries, climbed over and under furniture, and slid across the icy floors on their bellies.

"There they are!" Anna exclaimed, pointing to a group of snowgies scaling the drapes upstairs.

Kristoff held a finger to his lips. Silently, he sneaked up to the snowgies climbing on the curtains. In his hands, he carried an empty flour sack borrowed from the royal chef. Kristoff dove after the snowgies, hoping to capture them in the sack, but they were too quick for him. They jumped free of the drapes and scurried out of the sitting room, bounding down the hall. Kristoff and Anna took off after them.

"They're headed for the steps!" Kristoff shouted.

Up ahead was the main staircase. It led from the second floor down into the Great Hall, where Elsa and Olaf were still dining with the guests. If the snowgies reached the stairs, they were sure to interrupt the meal.

The little snowmen stopped when they came to the top of the steps. For a moment, Anna thought they might turn around and head in another direction. But she and Kristoff weren't that lucky. The snowgies gathered next to the banister post. One by one they climbed on top of each other's shoulders.

"They're like little acrobats!" Anna said, amazed.

The snowgies formed a wobbly tower with their bodies. Soon, the tower was the same height as the stair post.

"Uh-oh," Anna said. She had a bad feeling about what would happen next. Sure enough, more of the little snowmen began to gather at the steps. They climbed to the top of the shaky snowgie tower and hopped off onto the post. Then, one after the next, they slid down the banister, giggling happily.

"Looks like fun!" Kristoff said, caught up in the excitement.

"Kristoff," Anna said seriously. "Do

you know where those stairs lead?"

"To the Great Hall," he answered.

"And *who* are we supposed to keep out of the Great Hall?" asked Anna, reminding him of their goal.

"Right," Kristoff said. "Let's go."

Kristoff and Anna raced down the stairs as quickly and quietly as they could. They chased the snowgies across the far side of the Great Hall toward the chef's chamber.

"What in the world?" the chef exclaimed as a tide of snowgies poured into her makeshift kitchen. The tiny snowmen fanned out across the room, overturning pots and serving dishes. Then they circled the cooking assistants, running between their feet and accidentally tripping some of them. When Anna and Kristoff stumbled into the room moments later, the place was a complete mess.

"Oh no!" Anna groaned. She saw the snowgies jump one by one into a huge tub of vanilla ice cream.

"My dessert!" the chef shouted. The tiny snowmen waded happily through the sea of ice cream. They didn't seem to

notice the chef's distress. "Out! Out! Get them out!" she cried.

Anna and Kristoff ran over to the tub of ice cream. They reached in with their hands—much to the chef's dismay—and scooped out as many snowgies as they could. Unfortunately, the little snowmen were slippery. Covered in blobs of ice cream, they slid easily through Anna's and Kristoff's fingers. The snowgies scampered around the room, leaving tiny trails of ice cream–covered footprints.

Anna spotted a stack of white cloth napkins on the chef's table. She picked them up and tried to wipe the snowgies clean, but it didn't work. Instead, she only

succeeded in covering them head to toe with napkins as they wriggled out of her reach and ran off.

*

At the dining table, Mitya and Galina were more convinced than ever that something strange was going on in the ice palace. Elsa and Olaf were acting odd. Add to that the mystery of the overturned water glass and the phantom foot touch, and there was only one possible explanation.

"This place is haunted!" Mitya whispered to Galina.

Galina nodded nervously in agreement.

All of a sudden, Marshmallow trudged into the room. His ice cocoon had thawed. The moment he came indoors, Elsa asked him to help serve the tea. She was grateful for the distraction. With Marshmallow in the room, the ambassadors were less likely to notice anything else out of the ordinary.

Marshmallow carried a silver serving tray. It held a beautiful tea set made of ice, created with Elsa's magic. Each of the cups had a delicate snowflake pattern carved on the side. As Elsa poured the iced tea into the cups, Marshmallow balanced the tray carefully in his icy hands.

Suddenly, the door to the chef's chamber swung open with a crash! A swarm of snowgies scurried out of the

kitchen, completely covered in white cloth napkins. With the napkins over their heads they looked just like . . .

"GHOSTS!" Mitya and Galina shouted.

"Ghosts?" Elsa asked, confused. She peered at the parade of tiny phantoms. "Those aren't ghosts," she said, quickly recognizing the tiny snowmen. "They're—"

"SNOWGIES!" Kristoff yelled as he and Anna chased the napkin-covered snowmen into the Great Hall.

"Come back!" Olaf cried.

The snowgies couldn't see very well with the napkins covering their heads. They scattered blindly across the room, bumping into tables, chairs, and even Marshmallow. Marshmallow tried to move away from the confusion, but the snowgies ran under his feet. The giant snow monster tripped. He slipped backward, tossing the silver tray into the air. Marshmallow windmilled his arms as he fell, accidentally whacking the chandelier.

"Oh no!" Anna shouted, pointing to

the chandelier. The elaborate ice sculpture cracked and broke loose from the ceiling.

The ambassadors covered their heads with their arms to protect themselves, but there was no need. Elsa reached out with her powers. She extended her arms, channeled a powerful blast of ice through her fingertips, and froze the chandelier in midair! It hung suspended in a giant arc of ice. The arc stretched from one end of the Great Hall to the other like a frosty rainbow.

Mitya and Galina uncovered their heads just in time to see the snowgies wriggle out from under the napkins. The ambassadors started in surprise.

"So much for our ghosts," Galina said, astonished.

Mitya looked from Galina to the gaggle of bouncing snowgies surrounding him. He was so stunned that he fell backward and fainted.

Chapter 10

A short while later, Elsa and Anna explained all about the snowgies to the ambassadors.

"They came from your cold?" Mitya asked. Now that he was awake and understood that the castle wasn't haunted, he wanted to learn as much as he could about the little snowmen.

"That's right," Elsa answered. "They just sort of happened."

"They're delightful," Galina said. "Why didn't you tell us about them sooner?"

"I just wanted everything to be perfect for your visit," Elsa explained. "I was worried you might think the snowgies were a little odd."

"Odder than cold dinner in an ice palace?" Mitya asked lightheartedly.

"Point taken." Elsa laughed. And just like that she realized: the official welcome might not have gone as planned, but they were off to the start of a wonderful visit.

A few days later, it was time for Mitya and Galina to return to Vakretta. Everyone met in the Great Hall to see them off. This time the snowgies were in their proper place. Olaf lined them up so they stretched across the room. When he gave the signal, the snowgies jumped, one after the other, starting with the first snowman in line. The welcome wave was now a goodbye wave, and the ambassadors responded with friendly applause.

When the wave ended, Anna stepped forward. "Now that the snowgies have said their goodbyes, Elsa and I have a special surprise for you," she said.

"I'm not sure I can take another surprise," Mitya joked.

"I think you'll like this one," Anna told them. "In fact, I guarantee it."

Anna and Elsa helped the ambassadors into their cloaks and led them outside. The sky was a brilliant shade of blue and the sun shone through the clouds.

"It's beautiful here on the North Mountain," Galina said.

"We thought you might like to take a ride along the mountain trails," Anna explained.

"We'd love to," said Mitya, looking around. "But where's our sleigh?"

"That's the surprise," Elsa said. She raised her arms and sparkling crystals of ice swirled around her. Soon the frosty

crystals began to take shape. Elsa sculpted them into an elegant sleigh carved out of ice.

"That's incredible!" Galina exclaimed.

Anna put her fingers to her lips and blew a loud whistle. In response, Kristoff stepped out from behind a nearby tree, leading his reindeer, Sven, by the reins. He walked over to the sleigh and hitched Sven to it.

"All aboard!" Kristoff said, hopping into the driver's seat. The ambassadors climbed into the sleigh.

"Thank you for letting us borrow your lovely sleigh," Galina said.

"It's not for you to borrow," Elsa replied.

"It's a gift to the people of Vakretta."

"How can we ever repay you?" Mitya asked.

"Just come back and visit us sometime," Elsa said with a wink.

It was a trip the ambassadors from Vakretta would never forget.

*

After their guests had left, Anna and Elsa walked back inside the ice palace. With the ambassadors gone, they had time to relax—until Olaf bounded up to them.

"I see something that needs fixing," he said, pointing to the ceiling. The

chandelier still hung suspended in its arc of ice.

"Hmm," Anna said. "What are we going to do about that?"

"Whatever we do," Elsa said confidently, "I'm sure we can fix it together!"

© Jenn Carvin Photography

Erica David has written more than forty books and comics for young readers, including Marvel Adventures *Spider-Man: The Sinister Six.* She graduated from Princeton University and is an MFA candidate at the Writer's Foundry in Brooklyn. She has always had an interest in all things magical, fantastic, and frozen, which has led her to work for Nickelodeon, Marvel, and an ice cream parlor, respectively. She resides sometimes in Philadelphia and sometimes in New York, with a canine familiar named Skylar.